THIS LAND

THE FALL OF TĀNE

THE GRAPHIC NOVEL
BOOK TWO

BY **MARK ABNETT**

ART BY **P.R. DEDELIS**

SCHOLASTIC
AUCKLAND SYDNEY NEW YORK LONDON TORONTO
MEXICO CITY NEW DELHI HONG KONG

For Sindy.
With special thanks to Ben, Lenora,
Carlos, Logan, Eva & Delta.

Published in 2023 by Scholastic New Zealand Limited
Private Bag 94407, Botany, Auckland 2163

Scholastic Australia Pty Limited
PO Box 579, Gosford, NSW 2250, Australia

This book is an extended adaptation of issues 4 and 5 of the comic *This Land*,
published 2021-22 by Mark Abnett

ISBN 978-1-77543-792-5
Written by Mark Abnett
Art by P.R. Dedelis
Colouring by Liezl Buenaventura
Lettering by Rob Jones
Design of Beach character by Craig Peterson

Thanks to Verona-Meiana Putaranui for cultural guidance,
Trent Brown-Marsh for translation, Hekiera Mareroa, Seb Wikaraka Peni
and Te Haunia Tuna for their Māori visual art.

A full catalogue record for this book is available from the National Library of New Zealand.

10 9 8 7 6 5 4 3 2 1 3 4 5 6 7 8 9 / 2

Publishing Team: Lynette Evans, Penny Scown & Abby Haverkamp
Book design by Smartwork Creative www.smartworkcreative.co.nz
Printed in China by R R Donnelley

Scholastic New Zealand's policy is to use papers that are renewable and made efficiently from wood grown in responsibly managed forests, so as to minimise its environmental footprint.

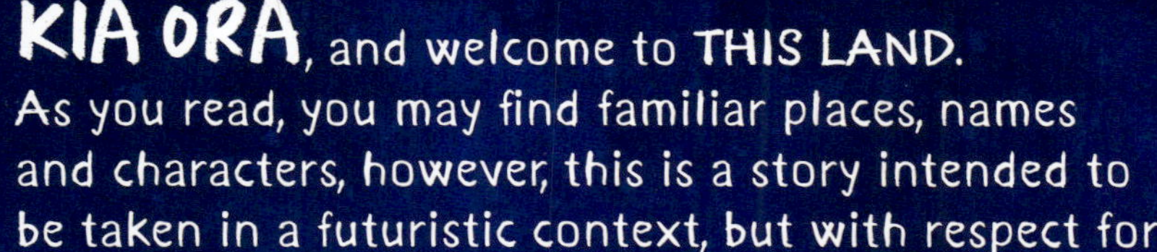

KIA ORA, and welcome to **THIS LAND**.
As you read, you may find familiar places, names and characters, however, this is a story intended to be taken in a futuristic context, but with respect for what has come before.

The artwork in this book is the visual interpretation of artists in creative and contemporary storytelling from around the world and Aotearoa New Zealand. We hope you enjoy this story and our depictions and designs of atua (gods) as we have imagined them.

MARK ABNETT

OUR JOURNEY CONTINUES WITHIN THE FUTURE REBORN WORLD OF AOTEAROA NEW ZEALAND.

52 YEARS HAVE PASSED SINCE THE BREAKING OF THE MOON AND THE DEATH OF TECHNOLOGY.

THE GODS HAVE BEEN SILENT FOR GENERATIONS.

BUT NOW THEY HAVE RETURNED.

AND THEY ARE NOT HAPPY WITH WHAT THEY HAVE FOUND.

KIA ORA, E HOA MĀ*!
HOWZIT GOING?
*Hello, friends
YOU'RE PROBABLY WONDERING WHY A WEE PĪWAKAWAKA* LIKE MYSELF IS NARRATING THE INTRO TO PART TWO OF THIS STORY. WELL, DON'T WORRY, I'VE BEEN ALONG FOR THE RIDE THE WHOLE TIME, BUT IF YOU'VE JUST JOINED US, HERE'S WHAT HAPPENED IN BOOK ONE.
*Fantail
SO, HERE WE ARE IN THE LAND OF TE RIU-A-MĀUI ...

IT'S A FUTURE AOTEAROA NEW ZEALAND, WHICH AROSE AFTER THE DESTRUCTION OF THE MOON CAUSED MASSIVE CHANGES IN THE WORLD'S TIDES AND TECTONIC PLATES, GIVING BIRTH TO THIS NEW LAND.
THE UPHEAVAL RELEASED A FEVER ACROSS THE LAND, CAUSING ITS PEOPLE TO EVOLVE WITH POWERS AND ABILITIES OF THE ATUA* AND, BOY, ARE THINGS CRAZY!
*Gods
ONE OF THOSE ATUA, TĀNE, CRASHED TO EARTH, TRAPPING THE FAMILY OF HELL'NA, A POWERFUL MEMBER OF THE PĀHUNU TRIBE OF AXELAND.

WHACK!
HELL'NA MANAGED TO KNOCK THIS ATUA OUT, BUT WAS THEN JAILED IN A PRISON IN AXELAND, ALONG WITH TĀNE, FOR MISUSE OF HER POWER.
TĀNE STRUCK A DEAL WITH HELL'NA TO RELEASE HER FAMILY IN EXCHANGE FOR HELPING HIM FIND THE DEMI-GOD MĀUI.
THEY BROKE OUT OF JAIL AND, WITH THE AID OF HER BROTHER'S CONTACTS, HELL'NA RECRUITED A SPECIAL GROUP OF MERCENARIES.

HELL'NA
WIELDER OF MANA STEEL, LIMITED FIRE MANIPULATION, DEFINITELY HAS IT ALL UNDER CONTROL, OR SO SHE THINKS.

TĀNE
SAYS HE'S AN 'ASPECT' OF TĀNE, GOD OF THE FOREST.

MOA
METAMORPH, SHAPESHIFTER, OVERPROTECTIVE FATHER OF TŪĪ.

TŪĪ
SPEED, FLIGHT, OPTIMIST.

MERE
ENERGY CHANNELLER, POUNAMU WELDER, ADDICT, ALL EGO.

PANIA
AXE WIELDER, STRATEGIC MASTERMIND, FIGHTS TO RELAX.

BEACH
SAND MANIPULATOR, WEAPON FORGER, LOSING HIMSELF ONE PIECE AT A TIME.

DRE
HELL'NA'S BROTHER, EX PRO KĪ-O-RAHI PLAYER, INVOLVED IN STUFF EVEN HELL'NA DOESN'T KNOW ABOUT.

LED BY THEIR WHITETOMB GUIDE, RANA, THEY JOURNEYED TO THE WAITOMO CAVES AND SEARCHED THE LIBRARIES OF THE UNDERGROUND CITY OF NEW ARANUI LOOKING FOR MĀUI.
HELL'NA ALSO USED THIS AS AN OPPORTUNITY TO ATTEMPT TO RESCUE HER FRIEND CHASE, WHO WAS BEING HELD BY THE WHITETOMB AGAINST HER WILL.
BUT CHECK THIS OUT! HELL'NA ACCIDENTALLY RELEASED A CAGED AND VERY HUNGRY TANIWHA* WHO BEGAN TO DESTROY THE CITY.
*Water dragon

RUUUUUUMMMMBLE!
TĀNE GIFTED A PORTION OF HIS POWER TO HELL'NA'S MASSIVE MATE MOA, WHO GREW INTO A GIANT KAIJU LEVAL MONSTER AND SACRIFICED HIS LIFE TO FIGHT OFF THE TANIWHA!

MEANTIME, TŪĪ AND PANIA HAD FOUND A CLUE TO MĀUI'S LAST KNOWN LOCATION - LAKE TAUPŌ.

AND, WOULD YOU BELIEVE, HELL'NA'S OWN AUNTIE HAD SENT THIS RIVAL GROUP OF MERCENARIES OUT TO STOP HER!

AND ONE OF THIS GROUP SEEMS TO KNOW HELL'NA QUITE WELL ... I WONDER WHAT THAT'S ALL ABOUT, EH?

KIRIANA
SHEPHERD, LEADER, TRACKER, FINDER OF LOST THINGS, HOLDS A GRUDGE

DUSTER
POUNAMU HUFFER, HEALING FACTOR, WIRED 24/7, ANGRY MAN

COMMISSIONER NGAIRE
LEADER OF THE AXELAND WARDENS & SECURITY, FULL OF SECRETS, HELL'NA'S AUNTIE.

MATAPARA
MUTE, THINKS HE'S A DEMIGOD, REALLY JUST A SALTY BIG FISH

VOX POPULI
VOICE OF THE WHITETOMB PEOPLE, PROPHET, SELF-SERVING, SPEAKS TO THE WORST PEOPLE, LOST AN ARM AND POSSIBLY MORE

KARLAKADA
INSECTOID, FLIGHT, INTERSPECIES COMMUNICATOR

MĀKUTU THE CURSED
A CREATURE OF DEAD THINGS, RE-ANIMATOR.
"IS HE EVEN ALIVE?"

REHU
EMPATH, PATHFINDER, PSYCHOMETRIST, HYPERCOGNITIVE, NO ONE BELIEVES HE KNOWS WHAT HE'S DOING

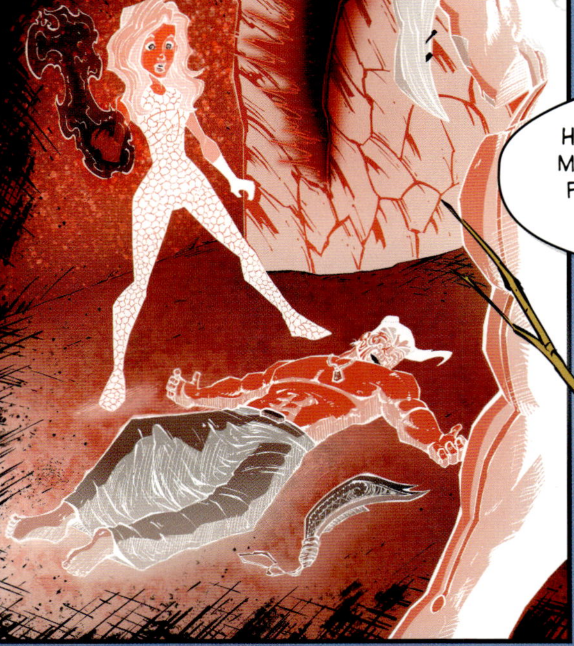
TĀNE AND HELL'NA WERE LAST SEEN AT THE BOTTOM OF LAKE TAUPŌ AT A GATEWAY TO THE UNDERWORLD, LOOKING AT THE FALLEN BODY OF MĀUI, WHO FOR SOME REASON LOOKS LIKE HELL'NA'S OLD FRIEND, LUKE!
THAT'S NUTS, RIGHT? HAS HELL'NA BEEN FRIENDS WITH MĀUI THIS WHOLE TIME WITHOUT EVEN KNOWING IT?
HE'S A CRAFTY ONE, THAT MĀUI. LET'S READ ON AND FIND OUT HOW THEY MET 15 YEARS AGO ...

TE-RIU-A-MĀUI

TAI-TONGA
TAI-RAWHITI
TAI-HAUAURA
TAI-TOKERAU
Tapu
Uncharted lands
Te Hono-i-Wairua
Gathering of
the Spirits
Whare Manawa
Jens Lake
Dunedin
Koura
Whiro's
Bay
Plain of 100 rivers
Queens Ruin
Ashburton
Otautahi
Wairuna Poke
Unclean Spirit
Chatham
Islands
Pa-raka-raka
Nelson
Wakanui
Mata Korpiri
Weta
Porirua
The Great Belt
Tuhua
Obsidian Plain
Green Door
Tatau Pounamu
Cameron
bunker
The Poke
Tongariro
Islands
Old Plymouth
Mokau
Bay of
Light
Lost House
Vegaspa
the Forge
Whitetomb
Lake of Glass
Pokeno
Trading
Post
Bombay Gorge
KIKORANGI
Ring
of Fire
Axeland
Mata
Mohiti
Hearts Flow
TAHI
RIMA
PANGO
MĀ
KŌWHAI
WHERO
WHĀ
600 mile beach
RUA
Five Fingers
of the Fever
TORU
KĀKARIKI

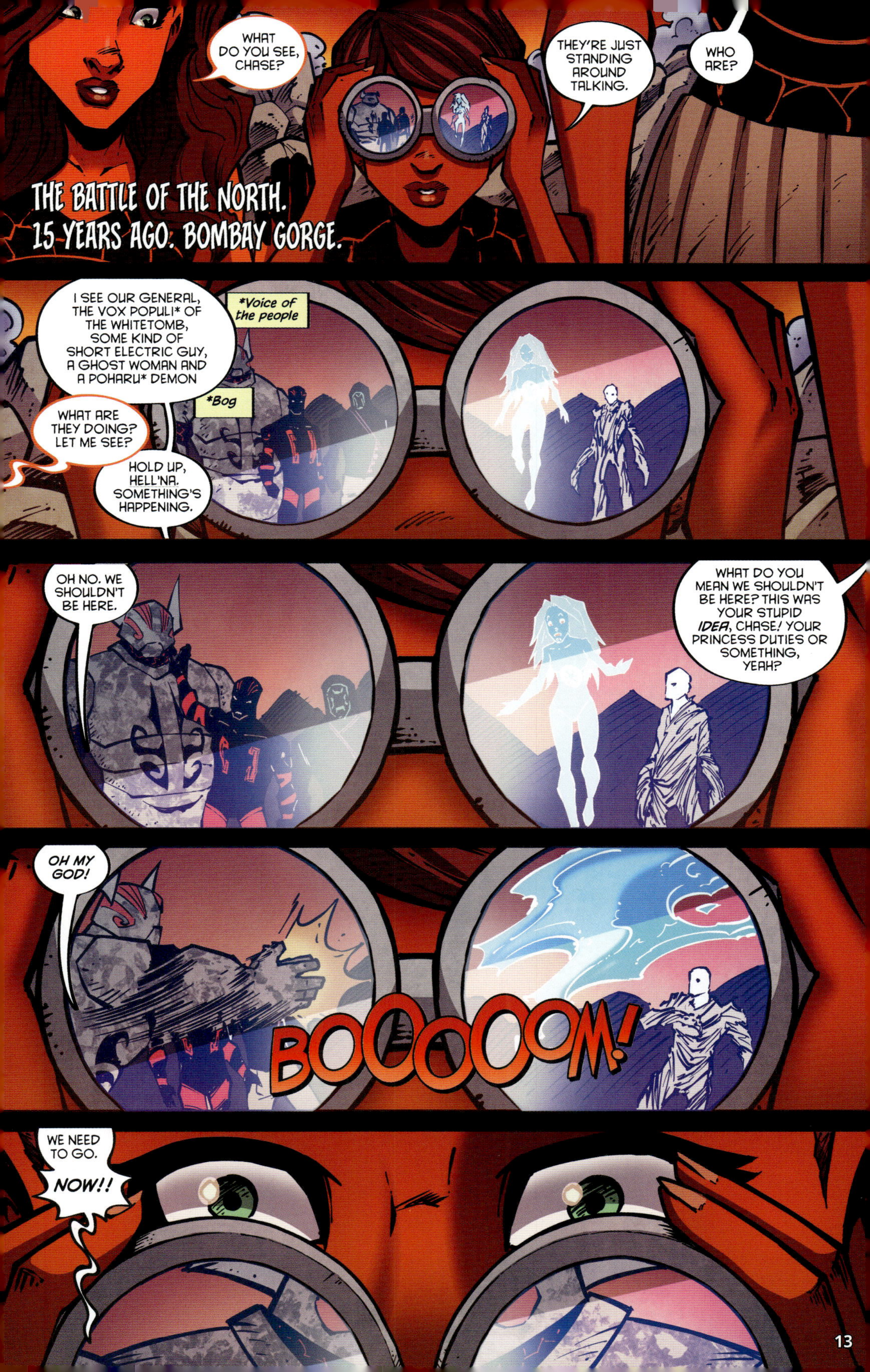
WHAT DO YOU SEE, CHASE?
THEY'RE JUST STANDING AROUND TALKING.
WHO ARE?
THE BATTLE OF THE NORTH.
15 YEARS AGO. BOMBAY GORGE.
I SEE OUR GENERAL, THE VOX POPULI* OF THE WHITETOMB, SOME KIND OF SHORT ELECTRIC GUY, A GHOST WOMAN AND A POHARU* DEMON
*Voice of the people
*Bog
WHAT ARE THEY DOING? LET ME SEE?
HOLD UP, HELL'NA. SOMETHING'S HAPPENING.
OH NO. WE SHOULDN'T BE HERE.
WHAT DO YOU MEAN WE SHOULDN'T BE HERE? THIS WAS YOUR STUPID IDEA, CHASE! YOUR PRINCESS DUTIES OR SOMETHING, YEAH?
OH MY GOD!
BOOOOOOM!
WE NEED TO GO.
NOW!!

AND THAT IS HOW THE WAR ENDED.
THE GREAT TREATY WAS SIGNED.
AXELAND WAS KEPT TO ITS BORDERS.

CHASE - THE DAUGHTER OF THE AXELAND KING (AND MY BEST FRIEND) - WAS PROMISED TO THE WHITETOMB AS A SYMBOL OF UNITY.
AND SO WE RAN.

EVEN THE SAFE HAVEN LAWS OF THE GREEN DOOR WERE CAST ASIDE AND WE WERE NO LONGER SAFE ON NEUTRAL GROUNDS.
WE DID WHAT WE COULD TO AVOID PATROLS AND BANDITS.
WE FOUGHT FOR EACH OTHER.
WE FOUGHT AGAINST EACH OTHER.
WE LOST ANA TO THE POHARU OF HELL'S GATE.
AND OF COURSE TEA RAN OFF WITH A PIRATE.

BY THE TIME **THE WHITETOMB** CAUGHT UP WITH CHASE AND ME, WE WERE LOST AND OUT OF OPTIONS.
IT TOOK THEM 18 MONTHS TO CATCH UP WITH US - AND JUST LIKE THAT MY FRIEND WAS GONE.
AND THERE I WAS...
AS FAR FROM HOME AS I COULD HAVE IMAGINED.
ALONE AND AFRAID.
AND IN ONE MOMENT MY LIFE CHANGED FOREVER.
WHAP!
KRAK!
I'D NEVER SEEN SOMEONE MOVE THAT FAST BEFORE. I'M STILL NOT SURE HOW SHE DID IT.

SHE SAVED ME.
AND SHE WASN'T ALONE... THERE WAS SOME GUY WITH A PONYTAIL.
THEY HAD A STRENGTH BETWEEN THEM AND MOVED WITH PURPOSE. BRUTAL AND POETIC.
THEY TAUGHT ME THE ART OF WAR.
THEY TAUGHT ME HOW TO SURVIVE.

BACK TO THE PRESENT... THE HOUSE OF THE DEAD
BUT I DON'T UNDERSTAND.
WHY DID YOU CALL HIM MĀUI?
THIS IS LUKE. THIS IS MY FRIEND.
HOW IS HE HERE?
NOW THAT IS A STORY.
WIFE.
UH... WHAT?
HUSBAND.
IT'S COMPLICATED.
HELL'NA, THIS IS HINE-NUI-TE-PŌ THE GODDESS OF DEATH.
I PREFER GODDESS OF THE NIGHT.

*Mother Earth
HUMANS BROKE THE MOON. PAPATŪĀNUKU'S* PLACE IN THE SKY MOVED AND THE GREAT NET THAT TOOK THE SOULS OF THE PEOPLE TO THE NEXT WORLD COULD NO LONGER REACH THIS LAND.
AND WHIRO? WELL, WHIRO FED. ALL THE DEATH, ALL THE WAR, HE CONSUMED IT ALL.
AND THE DOORS OF THE UNDERWORLD BROKE OPEN. TAI-WHETUKI, THE HOUSE OF DEATH, WAS EXPOSED.
YOUR CHOSEN ONE, THE DEMI-GOD MĀUI, STOOD HIS GROUND AND STRUCK WHIRO WITH A BLOW FROM HIS MAGICAL JAW BONE THAT WOKE ALL TEN HOUSES OF THE UNDERWORLD.
WHIRO JUST LAUGHED AND WITH ONE TOUCH MĀUI FELL WHERE HE LIES.

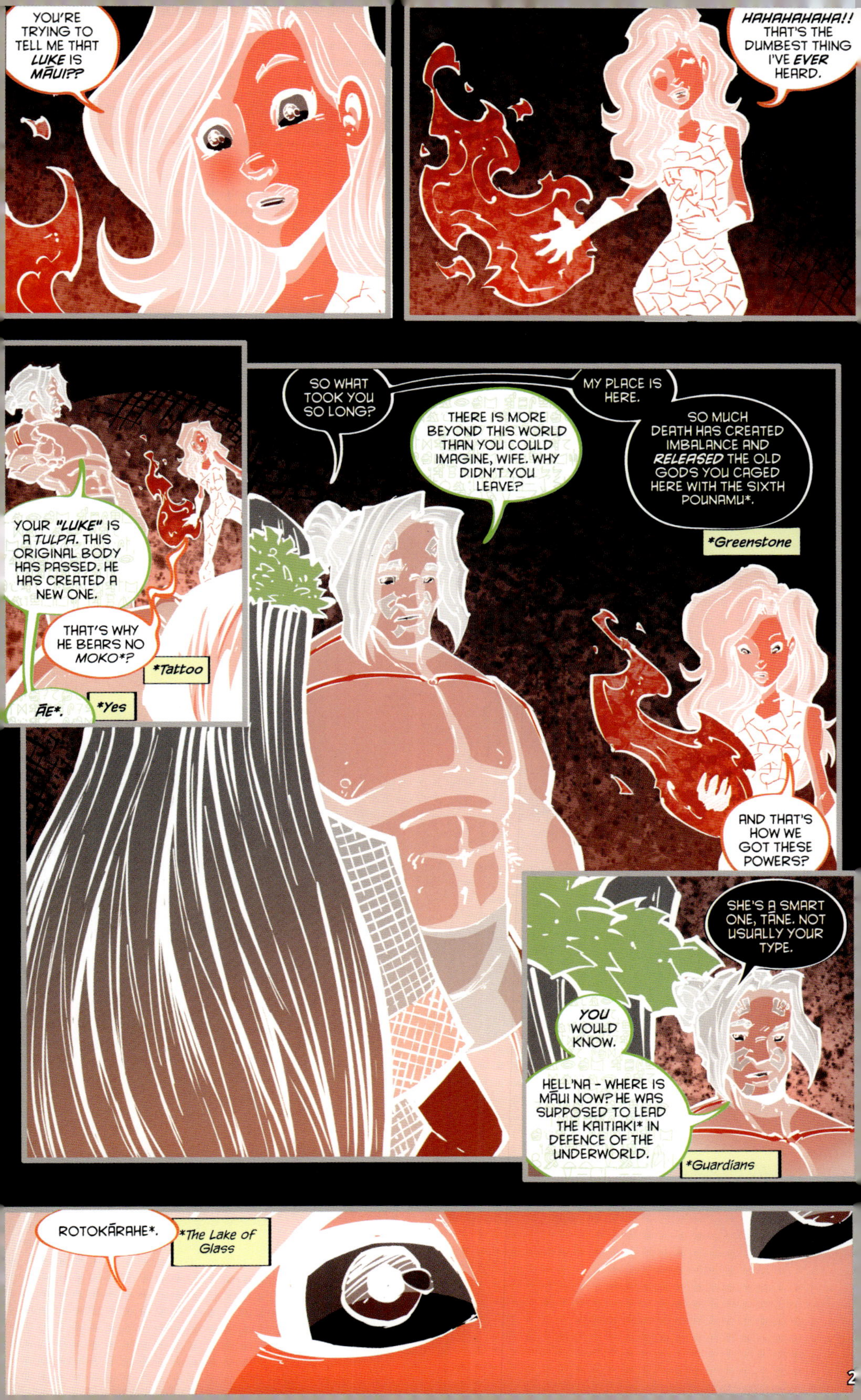

YOU'RE TRYING TO TELL ME THAT ***LUKE*** IS ***MĀUI??***

HAHAHAHAHA!! THAT'S THE DUMBEST THING I'VE ***EVER*** HEARD.

YOUR ***"LUKE"*** IS A *TULPA*. THIS ORIGINAL BODY HAS PASSED. HE HAS CREATED A NEW ONE.

THAT'S WHY HE BEARS NO *MOKO**?

**Tattoo*

ĀE*.

**Yes*

SO WHAT TOOK YOU SO LONG?

THERE IS MORE BEYOND THIS WORLD THAN YOU COULD IMAGINE, WIFE. WHY DIDN'T YOU LEAVE?

MY PLACE IS HERE.

SO MUCH DEATH HAS CREATED IMBALANCE AND ***RELEASED*** THE OLD GODS YOU CAGED HERE WITH THE SIXTH POUNAMU*.

**Greenstone*

AND THAT'S HOW WE GOT THESE POWERS?

SHE'S A SMART ONE, TĀNE. NOT USUALLY YOUR TYPE.

YOU WOULD KNOW.

HELL'NA - WHERE IS MĀUI NOW? HE WAS SUPPOSED TO LEAD THE KAITIAKI* IN DEFENCE OF THE UNDERWORLD.

**Guardians*

LAKE TAUPŌ
THE SHORE ABOVE
WHEN THIS IS ALL OVER, DO YOU THINK SHE'LL ACTUALLY HAVE THE MANA STEEL SHE OWES US?
YOU GIRLS THINK SHE'S GOING TO CHEAT US?
YEAH, NAH, YEAH, SHE WOULD BE *CRAZY* NOT TO PAY US.
AS SOON AS WE'RE DONE I'M HEADING TO WETA AND GETTING ME SOME MORE POUNAMU TO REINFORCE MY ARMOUR.
IF YOU DIDN'T ***CRUSH*** AND ***SNORT*** IT EVERY CHANCE YOU HAD, YOU WOULDN'T HAVE TO!
THAT STUFF'LL ***KILL YOU!***
THAT STUFF ***POWERS ME UP.***
WITHOUT THAT STUFF YOU ALL WOULDN'T BE HERE.
BESIDES, I KNOW MY LIMITS. I'M IN CONTROL.
I have seen what becomes of those who fall under the spell of the sixth Pounamu.
Mindless monsters full of rage.
This is not a path you should follow.
SOUNDS LIKE YOU'RE TALKING ABOUT YOUR LITTLE ARMY HERE, MATE. WHY ARE YOU KEEPING THEM ABOUT?

The mana steel will help me purchase land where I can revive my whānau* and live in peace.
*Family
The shores of my birthplace contain the memory of my people and they will be born anew.
YEAH?
GOOD LUCK WITH THAT.
TUI?
WHY DO YOU NEED THE MANA STEEL?
DAD WAS OUT HUNTING B-REX WHEN THE MARAUDERS CAME. BY THE TIME HE GOT BACK IT WAS TOO LATE.
I WAS YOUNG, AND WITH THE SHOCK OF IT ALL, I SHRANK AND HID.
AND I'VE NEVER BEEN ABLE TO GROW BACK SINCE.
THAT'S HARSH SIS.
MY FATHER'S WISHES WILL BE MADE TRUE. WE WILL BUILD A HOME FOR THOSE WHO HAVE NONE. FOR ORPHANS OF WHIRO'S WAR.
I JUST WANT A PLACE TO REST MY HEAD AND THEN ONTO THE NEXT JOB FOR ME.
I LOVE IT OUT HERE. I FEEL LIKE I'M GETTING STRONGER EVERY DAY.
I'M GLAD TO HEAR THAT.

LET'S PUT YOU TO THE TĒHI*!
*Test

THEN IT IS SETTLED. I WILL REMAIN AND WATCH OVER THE ENTRANCE. YOU WILL FIND MĀUI, GATHER THE KAITIAKI* AND DRAW OUT WHIRO.
*GUARDIANS

WE WILL NEED ALL THE *MANA** WE CAN GATHER.
*Spiritual power

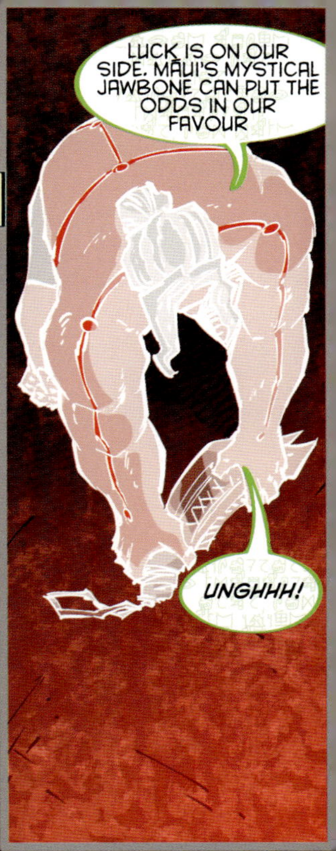
LUCK IS ON OUR SIDE. MĀUI'S MYSTICAL JAWBONE CAN PUT THE ODDS IN OUR FAVOUR
UNGHHH!

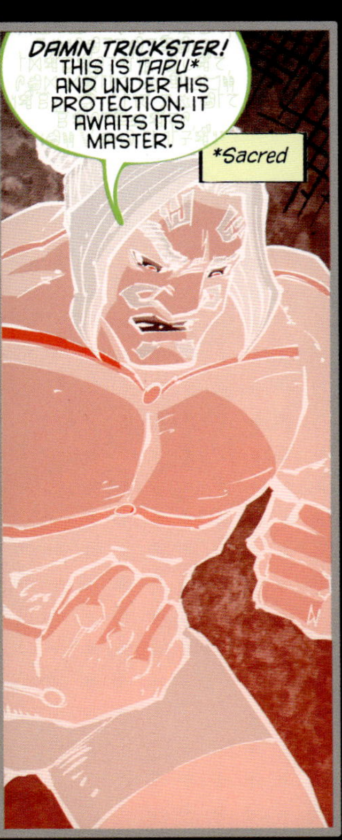
DAMN TRICKSTER! THIS IS *TAPU** AND UNDER HIS PROTECTION. IT AWAITS ITS MASTER.
*Sacred

I'LL GIVE IT A GO.
NO...YOU ARE NO ATUA*. IT WOULD DRIVE YOU TO MADNESS...WE ARE DONE HERE.
*God

WELL, THIS ISN'T THE TYPE OF REUNION I IMAGINED, H.
KIRIANA?
WHAT IN WHIRO'S NAME IS THIS?
OH, C'MON GIRL, DON'T BE LIKE THAT.
SOME OF US HAVE GOT BILLS TO PAY.
BESIDES YOU WERE NEVER REALLY ONE TO PICK UP THE TAB, NOW WERE YOU?
KIRIANA?
ARE YOU *KIDDING* ME?
YOU'RE RUNNING WITH *THIS* LOT FOR MONEY?
WHAT CAN I SAY? THAT AUNTIE OF YOURS PAYS WELL.

⇒SIGH⇐ OF COURSE SHE DOES.
NOTHING THAT WOMAN DOES SURPRISES ME ANYMORE.
SHE'S PROBABLY BEEN SIDING WITH WHIRO FROM THE START.
IT CAN'T BE?! IS THAT A KOHUKOHU*?
*Curse
RRRRRAAAAHHHHH!
STOP, YOU IDIOT!!
SKRACKK!
...
H! BEHIND YOU!

KAAAAAWWW!
YOU WANT TO KĀKARI*?!
*Fight
LET'S GO!

KKRACKK!
SPLASH!

OH, C'MON MATE. IT'S NOT A FAIR FIGHT, IS IT? LET ME GRAB MY GEAR AND WE DO THIS THE WAY TŪ INTENDED?
HOW 'BOUT *NO?*
YOU'RE A PSYCHIC, AREN'T YOU? BET YOU WON'T SEE *THIS* COMING!
THIS FIGHT WAS OVER BEFORE YOU WOKE THIS MORNING.

HOLD STILL, YA BLOODY PIXIE!
NOT ON YOUR LIFE, COCKROACH.
THANKS FOR LEADING US HERE, GLASSIE. YOU SHOULD KNOW BETTER THAN TO LEAVE PARTS OF YOURSELF BEHIND. WE'VE BEEN WATCHING THE WHOLE TIME.
And I've been watching back.

WHAT?!
THIS! THIS IS THE REAL POWER, BOY!
BURN...
GNAHH!!
GRRRRRR...

TIME TO GO, BOSS.
IT'S TRUE. HE IS TĀNE! WHERE ARE THE OTHERS?
TOAST.
WHAT THE HECK, TĀNE?!

YOU WERE IN TROUBLE. I GAVE YOU A GIFT AND YOU WON.
HELL'NA, OVER HERE!
HE NEEDS A HEALER.
I'VE NEVER SEEN SUCH RAGE.
IT COULD HAVE BEEN ME.
IT COULD HAVE BEEN...
HE'S PASSED OUT FROM THE PAIN.
WHERE'S BEACH?
I am here, but I am not all here.
DAMN! I'M SO SORRY BEACH. TĀNE, CHANGE HIM BACK.

KĀO* I CANNOT SPARE MY STRENGTH. WE MUST PREPARE FOR WHIRO - AND WE CANNOT DEFEAT HIM ALONE.
*NO
REHU HAS SLIPPED AWAY AS WELL. HE WILL REPORT BACK TO AXELAND AND AUNTIE WILL SEND EVERYONE AFTER US NOW.
BEACH, SEND YOUR CLONES TO SPREAD THE WORD TO ANYONE WHO WILL LISTEN.
TO EVERY TRIBE, EVERY IWI OF THIS LAND.
TELL THEM THE *GODS* ARE HERE.
TELL THEM THAT TĀNE CALLS THEM TO ROTOKARĀHE, THE LAKE OF GLASS.
TELL THEM THEIR *DESTINY* AWAITS THEM.
THOSE WHO ARE GREEDY AND SEEK WAR WILL COME - AND WHIRO WILL REVEAL HIMSELF.
AND THEN THE GUARDIANS AND I WILL SEND HIM BACK TO HIS DOMAIN AND RESTORE PEACE TO THIS PLACE.

LATER
FANCY TRICK THAT. HIDING OUR MANA STEEL PAYMENT WITHIN YOUR CLOAK. PITY IT'S GONE.
I'M GOOD FOR IT.
THE WAY I SEE IT, WE'VE COME THIS FAR. IT'D BE HEAHEA* NOT TO FINISH THE JOB.
*Crazy
HOW'S MERE?
WE MANAGED TO RUSTLE UP SOME HOROPITO* LEAVES WHICH WILL REDUCE THE SWELLING. HE'S STABLE FOR NOW.
*Pepper Tree
BUT HE WILL NEED EXPERT HELP SOON.

AND I DON'T KNOW WHAT TO MAKE OF BEACH. HALF HIS BODY IS LIKE MELTED GLASS AND HE'S *STILL* MANAGING TO MAKE IT MOVE.
BANG
LOOK OUT!!
CLEVER GIRL.
KRRRRRAAAKK

Where is her hand?
BEACH! GIVE HER COVER.
TŪĪ, FIND OUT WHERE THAT SHOT CAME FROM.
IS THAT A GREENSTONE BULLET?

WHAT WAS THAT?
THERE, ON THE RIDGE - I SEE THEM.
I SAID I'M OKAY!
CIRCLE AROUND. I'VE GOT AN IDEA.
GUYS? WHAT'S HAPPENING TO ME?
WAIT! GUYS!
WHY CAN'T YOU HEAR ME?
I CAN HEAR YOU.
COME, LET US TALK.

WHO SAID THAT?
WHAT IS THIS?
COME NOW, CHILD.
I HEARD YOU SOUGHT AN AUDIENCE WITH ME.
WHY ELSE WOULD YOU BE HERE?
WHIRO!
WHAT DO YOU WANT, YOU MONSTER?
WELL, THAT'S JUST UNFAIR. I AM JUST DOING WHAT I WAS MADE TO DO – A SIMPLE ATUA WITH SIMPLE NEEDS.
IT'S NOT MY FAULT YOUR PEOPLE CHOSE TO FEED ME TILL I WAS FULL. AND NOW I AM BURSTING AT THE SEAMS.
WHAT YOU SHOULD BE ASKING IS, WHY DID THEY SET ME FREE?
WHY DO THEY LET ME FEED?
WHY HAS IT TAKEN THE ATUA THIS LONG TO TRY AND COLLECT ME?
THEY ARE AFRAID.
AFRAID OF WHAT WOULD HAPPEN IF YOU CHALLENGED THEM.

IT IS NOT ME YOU SHOULD FEAR.
IT IS MY BROTHER, TĀNE..
HE WHO MADE YOU.
HE WHO TAUGHT YOU ONLY WHAT HE WANTED YOU TO KNOW.
ALWAYS PLAYING WITH HIS HUMANS, TOYING WITH YOUR SMALL LIVES IN HIS LITTLE GAMES.

HELLUVA SHOT, BOSS.
HOW COME HELL'NA COULDN'T STOP IT?

THAT FOOL COULDN'T STOP THE POUNAMU* TIP. SHE ALWAYS THINKS SHE KNOWS BEST, AND THAT OVERCONFIDENCE CAME BACK TO BITE HER.
*Greenstone

CLUNK
GOOD TRICK THAT.
LOVE THAT COLLAPSIBLE RIFLE OF YOURS.
CLICK
NOW, LET'S GET MOVING.
THEY WON'T BE DISTRACTED FOR LONG.
I'VE KNOWN THAT GIRL LONG ENOUGH TO KNOW SHE'S PROBABLY GOT HER NEW FRIENDS TWISTED ROUND HER LITTLE FINGER.
ALL SHE'S GOOD FOR IS TEASING AND PLAYING SILLY GAMES.

KRACK!
HUH?
REHU, CHECK IT OUT.
KARLA, AIR SUPPORT.

KACHOOOOOM!

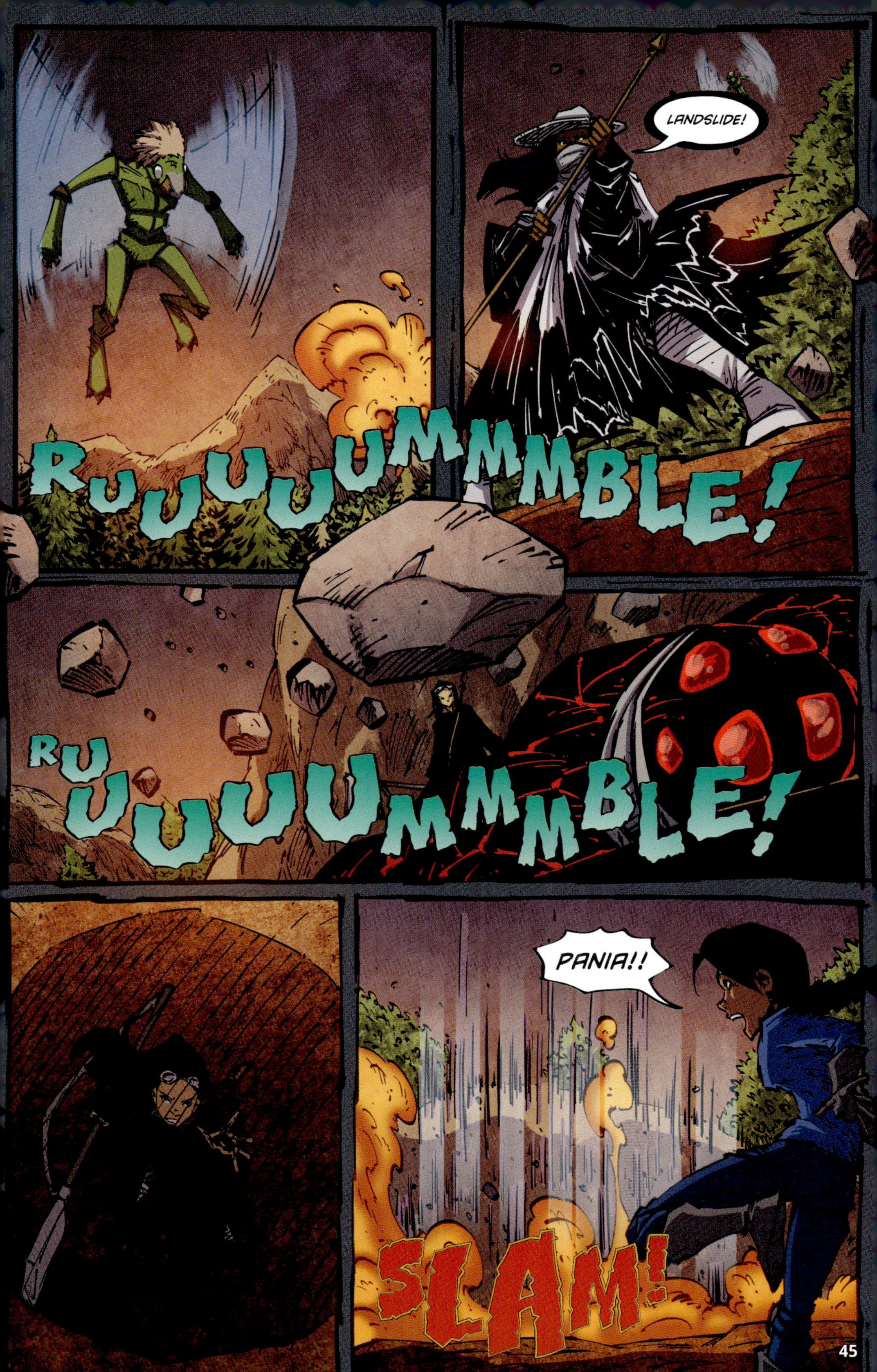

LANDSLIDE!

RUUUUMMMMBLE!

RUUUUUMMMBLE!

WHY DIDN'T YOU TELL ME YOU COULD MANIPULATE STONE?
A GIRL'S GOTTA KEEP SOME TRICKS TO HERSELF, YOU KNOW.
LET'S BOUNCE BEFORE THIS AMATEUR WAKES UP AND THEY FIGURE OUT WHAT'S HAPPENED.

DEEP IN HELL'NA'S MIND
HELL'NA.
COME.
SEE US.

WE ARE

HERE.
HELL'NA, WAKE UP!

5 KILOMETRES FROM THE LAKE OF GLASS
HEY, *THERE* SHE IS.
PARATA!* WHAT ARE YOU DOING HERE?
*Brother
WE GOT BEACH'S MESSAGE AT THE POKENO GREEN DOOR.
YARDIE SENT WORD AND I DECIDED TO GET THE BOYS BACK TOGETHER.
WAIT. WHO ARE ALL THESE *PEOPLE??*
WELL, JUST AFTER YOU AND THE GIRLS RAN OFF AFTER THE TRUCE, SOME OF US THOUGHT THAT PUTTING UP BORDERS BETWEEN IWI HAD NO PLACE.
SO THE FREE PEOPLE'S ARMY OF TE-RIU-A-MĀUI WAS BORN.
IT, AH, DIDN'T GO WELL.
BUT THINGS CHANGED AFTER YOUR LOT KICKED UP A MESS - BREAKING OUT OF AXELAND, BRINGING DOWN THE WHITETOMB AND TAMING A TANIWHA!
AND HAVING A REAL LIVE ATUA WITH YOU.
I THOUGHT YOU DIDN'T BELIEVE ME.
YEAH, WELL, THAT'S MY DUMB-ASS BEING OVER CAUTIOUS. IF GOOD OLD AUNT NGAIRE KNEW I WAS INVOLVED, THERE'S NO WAY YOU WOULD HAVE GOT THIS FAR.
AUNTIE?
WHY'S THAT?
KIDDO, YOU WOULDN'T BELIEVE WHAT THAT WAHINE* IS TIED UP IN.
*Woman

H! HOW'S THE HAND?
YOU NEVER TOLD US IT WAS A PROSTHETIC?
I SHOULDN'T HAVE TO. IT DOESN'T DEFINE ME.
WAIT, WHAT HAPPENED?
YOU BLACKED OUT.
BEACH SENT HIS DUPES OUT AFTER WHOEVER SHOT YOU AND CHASED THEM AWAY.
SEEMS TĀNE HERE HAS A BOUNTY ON HIS HEAD.
HUMPH.

"WE'VE GOT A LOT OF CATCHING UP TO DO."
SO YOU GOT WHAT YOU NEED.
NOW PAY UP.
I'VE LOST HALF MY CREW IN THIS JOB OF YOURS.
IT'S NOT EASY GETTING A KOHUKOHU AND A MATAPARA WORKING TOGETHER.
PAYMENT IS MADE ONCE THIS "GOD" IS BACK IN CUSTODY. WE HAVE NEW PLANS FOR HIM.
HELL'NA IS FOOLISH TO HEAD FOR THE LAKE OF GLASS. MY PEOPLE HAVE THE ADVANTAGE.
WITHOUT THE OTHER ELEMENTS TO AID THEM, HER COMPANIONS WILL BE DEFENCELESS AGAINST MY FORCES. THEY ARE SKILLED IN RONGO-MAMAU* AND WILL MAKE SHORT WORK OF THEM.
*Traditional Māori Wrestling
MAKE NO MISTAKE, SHEPHERD. THE ATUA WILL BE OURS. I HAVE THE WILL AND THE MANA TO MAKE IT HAPPEN.
ALL YOU NEED TO DO IS TAKE CARE OF HELL'NA LIKE YOU DID FOR ME ONCE BEFORE. DON'T LET ME DOWN LIKE THIS OLD FOOL BEHIND ME DID.
A DEAL'S A DEAL.

THE SHORES OF THE GLASS LAKE
TINO KORE NEI!*
*Absolutely no way!
MERE, IT'S THE ONLY WAY.
THE SIX OF US MUST GO TO THE CENTRE OF THE LAKE TO KŌRERO* WITH AUNTIE.
*Speak
IF WE CAN CONVINCE HER TO LEAD US TO WHIRO THERE WILL BE NO NEED TO FIGHT.
FORGET HIM, HELL'NA.
HE'S CAUSED US NOTHING BUT PROBLEMS THIS WHOLE TRIP.
NO, IT MUST BE ALL OF YOU.
*Bond
THE HONONGA* BETWEEN YOU ALL AND THE LINKS TO MY BROTHERS ARE ALL THAT WE NEED TO DEFEAT WHIRO.
WE NEED TO KEEP THE PEOPLES ARMY A SECRET FROM HER AS LONG AS POSSIBLE.
BETWEEN HER AND THE WHITETOMB THEY OUTNUMBER US THREE TO ONE. ANY ADVANTAGE WE HAVE IS A GOOD ONE.
EARN YOUR NAME, BROTHER.
KIA KAHA.*
*Be strong
TOGETHER THEN.

CENTRE OF THE LAKE OF GLASS
IT'S HIM.
THE ONE WHO STRUCK A DEAL TO HAND OVER CHASE

TĀNE!!!
NO!!
IT CAN'T BE!

TĀNE-MAHUTA, TĀNE-NUI-A-RANGI.
KO MAUNGAKIEKIE TE MAUNGA, KO TĀMAKI TE AWA, KO PĀHUNU TE IWI, KO AXELAND TE MARAE, KO NGAIRE PĀHUNU TOKU INGOA*, I CALL UPON YOU TO COME FORTH AND SURRENDER YOURSELF.
*Maungakiekie is my mountain, Tāmaki is my river, Pāhunu is my tribe, Axeland is my marae, Ngaire Pāhunu is my name.
YOU STUPID GIRL! YOU DON'T KNOW THE SACRIFICES THAT WERE MADE FOR THE SAKE OF PEACE.
WHERE WAS TĀNE WHEN THE FEVER CAME? WHERE WERE THE ATUA THAT SHAPED THESE LANDS?
ONLY WHIRO WAS HERE - AND THROUGH HIS VOICE WE CAME TO PEACE. AND LOOK WHERE WE ARE NOW...
YOUR ACTIONS IN THE WHITETOMB HAVE THROWN IT AWAY.
YOUR ANCESTORS WOULD BE ASHAMED. THEY SUFFERED AT WHIRO'S HANDS MORE THAN ANY PEOPLE.
INVASION, WAR, DISEASE... AND STILL THEY STOOD STRONG IN AROHA, MAHI AND MANA.

I CANT BELIEVE YOU, AUNTIE!
YOU TRADED MY FRIEND'S LIFE FOR THE TRUCE WITH THE WHITETOMB!
WHIRO KEPT ALL OUR BORDERS STRONG AND SAFE.
THE BODIES OF YOUR DEAD PROTECTED YOU. HE DIDN'T FOSTER WAR, HE HELPED KEEP THE PEACE.
WHERE IS YOUR TE AO MĀRAMA?*
*Wisdom and Understanding
AND WHERE IS WHIRO?
THE GREATEST ARMIES OF THE LAND STAND BEFORE ME, HOPING TO USE ME TO GAIN DOMINANCE OVER THE REST.
YOU ARE FOOLISH TO BELIEVE WHIRO WANTS TO HELP YOU. KEEPING YOURSELVES APART FOSTERS PREJUDICE AND HATRED - JUST WHAT WHIRO FEEDS ON.
WHERE ARE YOU, BROTHER?
SO SCARED OF *ME* YOU LET *OTHERS* DO YOUR WORK.
I...
AM...

EVERYWHERE!!
HHHHHHHH!
BOAHH

RRRRRRRARGH!
KABOOOOM!

KRAK

OOM!!

YOU COULDN'T EVEN SEE THAT I WAS TRYING TO SAVE YOU.
WHOSE IDEA DO YOU THINK IT WAS TO OFFER UP CHASE TO THE WHITETOMB?
WITH YOUR POWERS YOU'RE TOO VALUABLE TO AXELAND.
HELL'NA, I WAS PROTECTING YOU.
YOU DON'T GET IT, DO YOU? YOUR SELFISHNESS HAS ONLY LED TO OTHERS FALLING IN HARM'S WAY.
YOU CALL YOURSELF A LEADER.
YOU'RE JUST A TYRANT WHO WANTS TO CONTROL PEOPLE AND HOLD ONTO POWER. WE BROUGHT YOU ALL HERE TO DRAW HIM OUT. NOW LOOK!
WHIRO GROWS FROM THE DEATH AND DESTRUCTION YOU HAVE WROUGHT. HE WILL NOT STOP HERE.
HE WANTS TO SEE ALL OF TE RIU-A-MĀUI FALL.
WE ARE ALL ONE PEOPLE. THIS LAND HAS GIVEN US ANOTHER CHANCE.
LOOK, AUNTIE! OPEN YOUR EYES AND SEE WHAT'S IN FRONT OF YOU.
ALL THESE TRIBES FIGHTING – AND FOR WHAT? CONTROL OVER A GOD? THE GODS HAVE BEEN MANIPULATING US SINCE BEFORE THE FEVER.
WE MUST FIND OUR OWN PATH. TOGETHER, AS WHĀNAU.*
*Family
NO.

DAYS EARLIER...

KŌRERO*, TANE.

*Speak

BRING BACK TŪI'S FATHER AND I'LL PLEDGE MY LIFE TO YOU.

TO BRING ONE BACK, I MUST TRAVEL THROUGH THE HOUSES OF DEATH. WHEN THE TIME COMES, I ASK YOU TO SEND ME THERE.

WHAT TRICK IS THIS ?
NO TRICK. MY JOURNEY IS OVER.
MY PATH HERE GUIDED BY MY NEW WHĀNAU FOR A NEW WORLD.
I HAVE WITNESSED THEIR LOSS...
THEIR COURAGE...
THEIR WEAKNESS...
THEIR SELFLESSNESS...
AND THEIR *MANA.*
NOW ALL THAT REMAINS IS FOR YOU TO FACE THEM, MY BROTHER. FACE THE ***NEW GUARDIANS*** OF ***THIS LAND.***
FACE THE ***KAITIAKI****.
*Guardians

MY BROTHERS BARELY DEFEATED ME AND THEY WERE TRUE GODS.
HOW DO YOU THINK YOU WILL DEFEAT ME, E HINE*?
*Girl
TOGETHER.

INSIGNIFICANT FLEAS!
YOU DARE TOUCH ME?

GARRRGH!
NO, NOT LIKE THIS!!!
CURSE YOU, TANE!! CURSE YOU ALL...

THE REST OF THE BATTLE ENDED QUICKLY.
THE MEN AND WOMEN CAUGHT UNDER WHIRO'S SWAY SAID IT WAS LIKE A MIST BEING LIFTED FROM THEIR VISION.
OF COURSE THERE WERE THOSE WHO WOULD RETURN TO THE DARKNESS.
BUT THEIR NUMBERS HAD DWINDLED SO MUCH THAT THEY COULD OFFER LITTLE TO SUSTAIN WHIRO.

NO LONGER BLIND TO HATRED, THEY BEGAN TO EMBRACE ONE ANOTHER AS BROTHERS, SISTERS AND WHANAU.
SHARING THE BREATH OF A NEW DAY.
AND ONLY THEIR WEAKNESS REMAINED.
THERE WERE QUESTIONS LEFT UNANSWERED...
AND WORDS HAD GONE UNSAID.

WE EVENTUALLY WENT OUR SEPARATE WAYS. EACH LEFT WITH A PORTION OF THE POWER TĀNE HAD GRANTED FOR US.
IT GAVE SOME OF US HOPE.
IT GAVE OTHERS OPPORTUNITY...
AND FOR SOME IT WAS TOO MUCH TO BEAR.

AUNTIE TURNED HERSELF IN AND HAS NOT SPOKEN A WORD SINCE.
WE DON'T KNOW FOR SURE HOW MUCH WHIRO PLAYED A PART IN HER ACTIONS AND HOW MUCH WAS HER OWN DOING.
DRE WAS OFFERED A ROLE AS AN ADVISOR TO THE OPEN BORDER POLICE. HE TURNED IT DOWN BUT SAID HE WOULD COME URGENTLY IF NEEDED.
AS FOR ME, I FULFILLED MY PROMISE TO MY WHĀNAU AND USED MY PORTION OF POWER TO BRING BACK OUR TAMARIKI.*
*Children
THAT WAS TĀNE'S GIFT TO US - THE CHANCE FOR NEW BEGINNINGS.
A CHANCE TO USE THESE GIFTS TOGETHER AS ONE PEOPLE.

AND YOU KNOW WHAT? I THINK OUR WORK HAS JUST BEGUN.
WAIHO I TE TOIPOTO, KAUA I TE TOIROA.
LET US KEEP CLOSE TOGETHER, NOT FAR APART.
HEI KONEI KA MUTU...
THE END...
OR IS IT?

BEHIND THE SCENES OF
THIS LAND

THE GUARDIANS

When Tāne's journey is complete, he imbues the essence of his godly power into Hell'na and her friends, enabling them to evolve into Kaitiaki – the Guardians.

HELL'NA

Gifted the powers of Rūaumoko, god of earthquakes and volcanoes.

Hell'na's evolved form includes the circular porowhita symbol representing the never-ending circle of life. She can generate incredibly powerful heat blasts and manipulate the temperature of the air around her, allowing her the ability of flight.

BEACH

Gifted with the powers of Tangaroa, god of the sea.

Beach draws power from the grains of sand crushed on the shores of Te-Rui-a-Māui. Their memories combine to form powerful blasts and the manipulation of material formed by the grains.

His evolved form is covered in layers of sand that have seen generations of turmoil as the sea fought for its place against the shore.

MERE

Gifted the powers of Tū. god of people and war.

Mere's new form comprises an exoskeleton of energy channelling the rage and mana of Tū, the perfect form for combat, protecting its wearer from physical blows and giving him the ability to redirect kinetic energy into physical strength.

WARNING: If the wearer absorbs too much energy, the rage of Tū could drive them mad.

PANIA

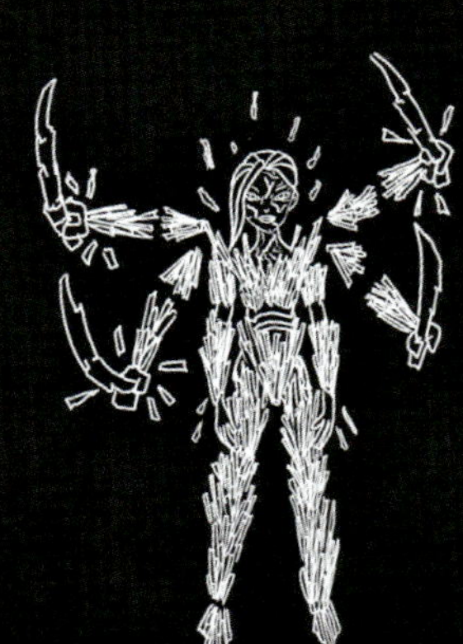

Gifted the powers of Tāwhirimātea, god of wind and weather.

The four extra arms of her evolved form represent the four winds. They carry various weapons forged from her body with the stone carved by those winds. These arms protect her from all sides, making it near impossible to perform a sneak attack on her.

Gifted the powers of Tāne-mahuta, god of forests and birds.

Tūī's evolved form is that of a giant kārearea (New Zealand falcon); an energy form that draws power from all the birds of Te-Riu-a-Māui. Her powerful wings could extinguish the strongest wildfires.

TĀNE'S TĀ MOKO

When the tulpa of Tāne reaches the end of his journey he develops a fully formed mataora facial tattoo. Traditionally, Māori men receive a mataora on their face as the head is sacred to Māori, therefore facial tattoos bear special significance. Tā moko (tattoos) reflect a person's whakapapa (ancestry) and personal history. In earlier times, it was indicative of social rank, knowledge, skill and eligibility to marry.

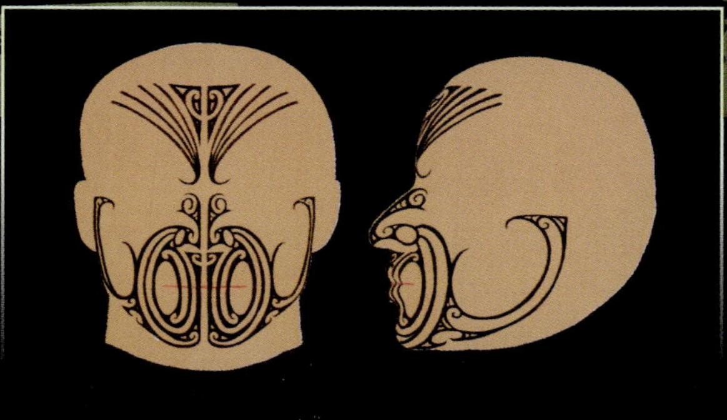

SYMBOLS USED IN THIS LAND

PĀHUNU (FIRE)

Similar to the Mangopare koru design, which represents the hammerhead shark, the Pāhunu symbol mimics the shape of a flame and represents strength and courage.

Used by the Pāhunu tribe, to which Hell'na and Chase belong.

THE WHITETOMB

The downward direction of this design symbolises the caves of Waitomo. It represents water flowing from a waterfall, and the hook is the rolling water beneath. It is inspired by an Indian symbol similar in design and meaning, as the majority of Whitetomb people are Tauiwi (visitors to Aotearoa) from many cultures around the world, who were trapped during the time of the Fever.

Vox Populi and Rana are from the Whitetomb.

TEWHATEWHA

The axe-head shape represents Tūmatauenga, the god of war. The symbol represents a weapon known as a *tewhatewha*, a long-handled Māori club shaped like an axe, wielded with two hands. Those who bear the mark of the axehead are those with no iwi or community, the followers of Tūmatauenga (Tū, god of war). Those who honour Tū claim his power for their own mana (honour) and their own protection. But there are those who abuse the symbol – gangs of outcasts, like Jack the Blade, who roam the lands sowing the seeds of chaos and destruction. They follow Whiro-te-tipua, the lord of darkness and embodiment of all evil. Whiro is their guide. He whispers in the ears of the weak, offering power and protection.

The tewhatewha is Pānia's weapon of choice.

KOWHAIWHAI design

This is the pattern used in the background of the THIS LAND title.

PIKORUA (single twist)

Representing the eternally intertwining paths in life, pikorua is a symbol of the strength of the bond between two people and their love, loyalty and friendship. No matter what divergent paths they may take, they will always be connected and shall return to each other.

POROWHITA (circle)

The porowhita represents the circle of life – the belief that life has no beginning or end. It also symbolises the cyclical nature of the world, seasons, relationships, a never-ending journey of discovery.

PIKORUA (triple twist)

Represents the bond between peoples and cultures, given as an offering of friendship between different peoples or tribes to signify an enduring connection.

ROIMATA (teardrop)

A stylised version of the toki, it is a comfort stone for healing, reassurance and positive energy, symbolising strength, power, pride and independence.

TOKI (adze)

Worn as a symbol of strength, the toki carries with it deep symbolism associated with mana, strength, determination and control.

DID YOU SPOT THESE CLUES?

MĀUI, IN THE FORM OF A PĪWAKAWAKA, HAS BEEN WATCHING THE WHOLE TIME . . .

Book one, page 64

Book two, page 22

Book two, page 22

Book two, page 26

Book two, page 30

Book two, page 31

Book two, page 36

Book two, page 38

Book two, page 53

Book two, page 59

Book two, page 59

Book two, page 73

Book two, page 74

DID YOU SPOT THESE CHARACTERS?

Jack the Blade at the Pokeno Tavern.
Book one, page 30

Kiriana in the tavern.
Book one, page 31

Jack the Blade talking to a Beach clone.
Book two, page 35

Jack the Blade getting arrested again!
Book two, page 70-71

DID YOU RECOGNISE THESE LOCATIONS?

Auckland Sky Tower.
Book one, page 20

Waitomo Caves visitor centre.
Book one, page 49

DID YOU NOTICE?

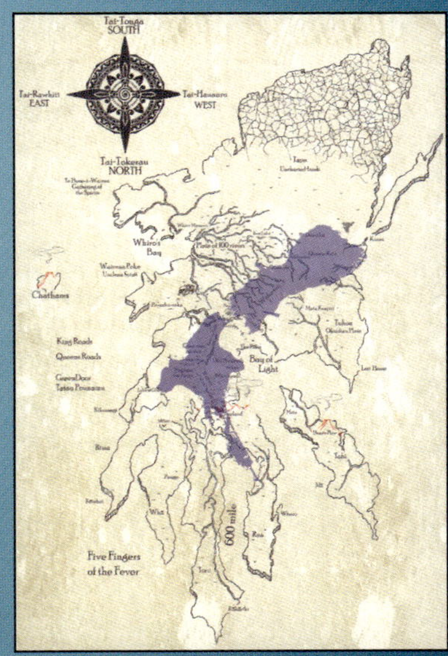

The map of Te Riu-a-Māui runs
South to North over Aotearoa

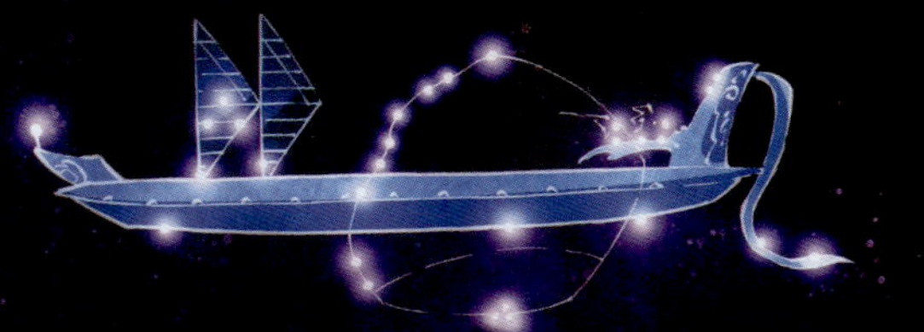

Did you spot the waka in the skies above Te Riu-a-Māui, with the star Matariki guiding the way?

CREATORS

MARK ABNETT - *Writer/Creator*

Mark is a New Zealander based in Scotland. He won the Netflix-owned Millarworld Talent contest in 2016. He's inspired by storytelling that's important to the identity of all Aotearoa, whether Māori, Pākehā or Tauiwi. Mark can often be found on his couch complaining about the weather and pining for a can of L&P.

P.R. DEDELIS - *Illustrator*

P.R. is an artist from Poland who's been drawing since reading his first Donald Duck comic book at the age of five. Since then he hasn't stopped, and has been drawing professionally for over a decade, working on titles like *5 Seconds*, *Word Smith*, *Team Synergy* and many more.

LIEZL BUENAVENTURA - *Colourist*

Liezl is a comic colourist and writer from Manila, Philippines. Over the years she has coloured a variety of titles, such as *Stabbity Bunny*, *Shadow Play*, *The Theory* and *Grimm's Fairy Tales: No Tomorrow*. In her spare time, she plays video games with her young son. He always wins.

ROB JONES - *Letterer*

Rob Jones is an award-nominated writer and award-winning letterer of comics. His credits include work for Image, Penguin Books, Humanoids, Heavy Metal, Scout, Behemoth, DC Thomson and on a multitude of small press and independent titles. He's a Brit who can be found shouting at the ducks in the local park.

VERONA-MEIANA PUTARANUI - Guidance

Verona is Te Aitanga ā Hauiti, Ngāti Porou, Rongowhakaata, Ngāi Tamanuhiri and Ngāti Pāhauwera. She is a Māori communications and engagement practitioner working with government and iwi.

HEKIERA MAREROA - Kowhaiwhai Design

Ko Konaki te maunga, ko Harataunga te awa, Ngati Porou ki Harataunga te iwi, ko Hekiera Mareroa ahau.

Hekiera is the marketing manager for Driving Creek, mostly known for its pottery, but also many other forms of art that continue to inspire him to create. Over the past few years Hekiera has studied the art of tā moko and kowhaiwhai, which he interprets on a digital platform. See kowhaiwhai (p.78).

SEB WIKARAKA PENI - Iwi Design

Ngāti Te Ngakau Seb holds a BA in Māori visual art. His influences are Cliff Whiting, Steven Gibbs and Sofia Minson, to name a few. Seb created the tribal symbols for This Land (p.78).

TRENT BROWN-MARSH - Te Reo Māori Translator

Trent is of Ngaati-Tipa and Ngaati Kaiaua descent of the Waikato Tribal Confederation. He is a cultural practitioner who aspires to the teachings of his tīpuna (ancestors) and is currently discovering comics for the first time.

TE HAUNUI TUNA - Tā Moko Artist

Te Haunui, of Ngāi Tuhoe, grew up in Waimana and now lives in Whakatāne. His work is inspired by his Māori heritage; it often depicts atua Māori, and frequently represents whakapapa. Te Haunui designed Māui's moko (p.77). He enjoys tattooing, painting, sculpting and drawing.

ARTISTS' CHARACTER INTERPRETATIONS

ARTIST: MICHEL MULIPOLA

HELL'NA

ARTISTS: ZAC HOWARD AND LIEZL BUENAVENTURA

BEACH

ARTISTS: CRAIG PETERSEN AND LIEZL BUENAVENTURA

RANA

ARTIST: LEO ART BRO

MERE

ARTIST: DAN TAUA

TĀNE

ARTIST: STORY HEMI-MOREHOUSE

"WOW! THIS LAND IS A GRAPHIC NOVEL BRINGING TOGETHER WELL-KNOWN PLACE NAMES OF AOTEAROA, SUPERPOWERS, MĀORITANGA AND A CHANCE TO LEARN SOME BASIC DAY-TO-DAY TE REO MĀORI (MĀORI LANGUAGE). THIS POWER-PACKED, ALL-OUT-ACTION READ IS WRITTEN FOR NOT ONLY NEW ZEALAND READERS BUT GRAPHIC NOVEL ADVENTURE FANS AROUND THE WORLD."
—WHATBOOKNEXT.COM

THANK YOU

Tēnā koutou. If you are holding this book in your hands, it is thanks to the many people who have helped make this a reality:

Sindy, Jen, Verona, Ben, Lenora, Carlos, Logan, Eva, Delta, Adam, Ellen, Rex and Molly … thanks for the support making the Awesome Sauce.

My fellow partners in creation: P.R. Dedelis, Liezl Buenaventura, Rob Jones, Hassan Otsmane-Elhaou, Verona-Meiana Putaranui, Hekiera Mareroa, Seb Wikaraka Peni, Trent Brown Marsh, Te Haunui Tuna and everyone else who contributed art, pin-ups and covers.

Lastly, the team at Scholastic – Lynette, Penny and Abby – and Erin from Smartwork Creative.

Wow, this thing is real because you chose to make it so. All the aroha in the world to you.

MARK ABNETT

ACKNOWLEDGEMENT

The sketch by P.R. Dedelis of the great waka on pages 20 and 81 is based on the art of Te Haunui Tuna for the book *Matariki: Star of the Year*, by Professor Rangi Matamua (Huia Publishers, 2017) and is represented here with the permission of both the author and the artist.

Matariki is the Māori name of the *Pleiades* star cluster, as well as being the name of one of the stars in the cluster, and the name of the celebration of its first rising in Aotearoa in late June or early July every year. This marks the beginning of the New Year in the Māori lunar calendar. Matariki sits at the head of the canoe Te Waka o Rangi, which is said to collect the souls of those who pass into the afterlife. In THIS LAND, with the upheavals on the Earth and the chaos in the skies above Te Riu-a-Māui, this no longer takes place … leaving Whiro free to feed from those souls.